MYSTERY of the WITCH'S SHOES

where?

Written by Robyn Supraner

Illustrated by Margot Apple

Troll Associates

Troll Associates, Mahwah, N.J.

Library of Congress Catalog Card Number: 78-60125
ISBN 0-89375-078-6

MYSTERY of the WITCH'S SHOES

Molly had no one to play with.

Carol was at the dentist's office.

Rhoda was visiting her grandfather.

And Stanley was shopping with his mother.

So Molly played *Pretend*.

She pretended she was a great tennis player.

She pretended she was a spy on a secret
mission.

She pretended she was being chased by
a wicked old witch.

She ran and ran and ran. When she stopped running, she was standing in front of a strange old house.

She decided to find out who lived there.
So she walked up the crooked path to the
front door.

She raised the knocker, and knocked twice. "Come in!" called a voice.

Molly pushed the door open and went inside.

The house was dark and gloomy. A candle flickered on the mantle. A raven perched on the back of a chair. A spider scurried to the center of its web and waited.

Molly shivered. Her ears tingled. The back of her neck felt creepy-crawly.

"I think I had better go home," said Molly.

"Please don't go," said the voice.

"Why not?" asked Molly.

"Because," replied the voice, "I can't find my shoes."

Molly looked behind the chair. A girl,
about her own age, was on the floor.
She was looking for something under the
sofa.

"I don't understand it," she said to
Molly. "I had them yesterday. Now I can't

find them anywhere. They are gone. They've
disappeared. Vanished into thin air. Who are
you?"

"I am Molly Muldoon," answered Molly.

"I am Maggie," said the girl. "I am a
witch."

"How do you do?" said Molly, for she had not forgotten her manners. "Are you a real witch?"

"Of course," said Maggie. "Now, will you please help me find my shoes before my mother gets home?"

"Is your mother a real witch, too?" asked Molly.

"My mother is a real witch. My mother's mother is a real witch. My mother's mother's mother is a real witch. We are all real witches," said Maggie. "Now, will you help me find my shoes?"

"If you really are a real witch," said Molly, "why don't you just say *hocus pocus, shoes appear!*"

"I can't," said Maggie. "I am being punished. My mother took away my magic."

"Why?" asked Molly. "Why did she do that?"

"I lose things," replied Maggie. "It's a terrible habit. I lost my broom. I lost my crystal ball. I even lost Sunshine. Now I've lost my new shoes, too. My mother says if I don't find them before she gets home, she is going to take away my magic for a hundred years!"

"That's some punishment," said Molly. "I will help you look for them."

"Look for them!" scolded the raven. He fluttered into the air and settled on Maggie's shoulder.

They looked in the cellar. A pair of small
gray mice scampered across Molly's feet.

"Sorry," said the first mouse.

"Beg your pardon," said the second.

"Have you seen my shoes?" asked
Maggie.

"We haven't seen them," said the first mouse.

"But we know where they are," squeaked the second.

"Yes," said the first. "We know where they are!"

"Well, tell me for goodness' sake!" said Maggie. "Where are they?"

"They are exactly . . ." squeaked the first mouse.

"Exactly where?" cried Maggie.

"Exactly where you left them!" giggled the second mouse. Then both little mice disappeared through a hole in the wall.

"What rude little mice!" said Maggie.

"Rude little mice!" croaked the raven.

"Never mind," said Molly. "Let's look upstairs."

They looked in the kitchen. They looked under the sink. They looked under the stove. They even looked in the refrigerator.

"What's that?" asked Molly.

"It's only a broom closet," said Maggie.

Molly opened it anyway. She saw a dust pan and a dust rag and dust mop. She saw beeswax and turtle wax and lizard wax. She saw a bottle marked Toads' Tongues and a

jar marked Bats' Ears. In the corner, she
saw a small broom.

"What a cute little broom," said Molly.

"My broom!" cried Maggie. "My magic
broom!" She grabbed the broom from Molly
and waltzed it around the kitchen. "It is
exactly where I left it!"

"We told you so!" squeaked the mice,
who had popped out of the wall.

"That's all well and good," said Maggie.
"But it doesn't find my new shoes."
    "Find those shoes!" scolded the raven.
    They looked in the dining room. There
were candlesticks on the sideboard, and vats

and vials in the cupboard. There was a
cauldron on top of the table.

"What is that furry thing hanging down
from the chandelier?" asked Molly.

"It's Sunshine!" cried Maggie. "I would
know her tail any place!"

Sunshine was very angry at having been left so long in the chandelier. She hissed and spit and arched her back.

"You know," said Maggie, "that is exactly where I left her."

"What did we tell you?" said the first mouse, who was nibbling on a piece of cheese.

"Listen and learn," squeaked the second, who was munching on a large purple grape.

"It's rude to talk with food in your mouth," said Maggie. "And besides, I still haven't found my new shoes."

"Time is wasting!" croaked the raven. "Your mother will soon be home!"

They hurried to the library. There were books about hexes and books about spells. There were notions and lotions and poison potions. And, on a cluttered table, an evil-smelling brew boiled and bubbled in an iron pot.

"What's that?" asked Molly. She pointed to a shining ball, half hidden by books and papers.

"My crystal ball!" cried Maggie. "Now I remember! It is exactly where I left it!"

"It is just as I said," squeaked the first mouse.

"It is just as *we* said," corrected the second.

"If you are both so smart," said Maggie, "tell me where to find my new shoes!"

"Where did you leave them?" asked the second mouse.

"That is where you will find them!" squeaked the first.

"Oh, dear!" cried Maggie. "I will *never* find them in time!"

"Hurry!" warned the raven. "No time! No time!"

"Think!" said Molly. "You said you had them yesterday."

"I did," said Maggie. "I had them on when I went to Aunt Hattie's for some spotted cucumber beetles. It was raining, so I wore my rubber boots. I remember, because the boots were too small. It was hard to pull them over my shoes."

"What happened when you came home?" asked Molly.

"I hung up my cloak, and put my boots in the closet. Then I went to the kitchen to brew a cup of sneezeweed tea. I didn't want to catch a cold," she explained. "Witches are very sensitive to chills."

"Were you wearing your shoes?" asked Molly.

"I think so," said Maggie. "I don't remember."

"Let's look in the hall closet," said Molly.

"It's no use," said Maggie. "They're not there. I've already looked."

"Let's look again," said Molly.

"Look again!" ordered the raven.

There were boots and rubbers and
pointy hats. There were capes and cloaks
and scary things.

"I don't see my shoes," said Maggie.

Molly took a pair of moleskin boots
from the closet. She took out a pair of toad-
skin boots. She took out a pair of snakeskin
boots. Then she took out Maggie's rubber
boots.

"That's strange," said Molly. "These boots are much heavier than the others." She put her hand in one of the boots. "Something is inside!" she said.

"My shoe!" cried Maggie. "My new shoe! Now I remember. My shoes got stuck when I took off my boots. They were in the closet all the time!"

"Exactly where you left them," said the first mouse. He looked around for the

Exactly

second mouse. "Oh, dear!" he squeaked.
"Where in the world is Penelope?"

"Exactly where you left her!" said
Maggie and Molly together.

"Exactly!" screamed the raven. And he
laughed until his feathers flew.

Just then, the front door blew open. The candles flickered. The raven hid his head under his wing. Sunshine arched her back and yowled like a Halloween cat.

"I would like you to meet my mother,"
said Maggie.

"How do you do?" said Molly.

"I do as I please," replied the witch.
Then she turned to Maggie and said, "Well,
my dear—have you found your shoes?"

"Yes," said Maggie. "And I found my broom and my crystal ball and my darling Sunshine, too. But I could not have found them without the help of wonderful Molly Muldoon."

"Then you must come with me, my dear," said the witch to Molly. "You must have a slice of creature cake and a glass of broccoli juice."

"No thank you," said Molly. "It's getting late. It is time for me to go home."

"Just a tiny sip of broccoli juice?" coaxed the witch. "It turns your cheeks the loveliest green."

"Some other time, perhaps," said Molly. "But thank you all the same."

Then she said goodbye to Maggie and to Maggie's mother and to Sunshine and the raven. And to Gustav (the first mouse) and Penelope (who was found).

"Goodbye, goodbye. Come back and visit us," they all called. And Molly thought that some day, perhaps she would.